Modern Curriculum Press
· BEGINNING
TO
READ
Series

The
Magic
Beans

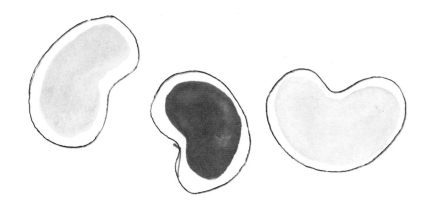

The Magic Beans

Margaret Hillert

Illustrated by Mel Pekarsky

MODERN CURRICULUM PRESS
Cleveland • Toronto

Library of Congress Catalog Card Number: AC 66-10514

ISBN 0-8136-5553-6 (Paperback)
ISBN 0-8136-5053-4 (Hardcover)

1 2 3 4 5 6 7 8 9 10   92 93 94 95

Oh, look.

Here is something funny.

One is red.

One is blue.

One is yellow.

One little one.

Two little ones.

Three little ones.

Look, look, look.

Go down here.

Go down in here, little ones.

Oh, oh.

Look and see.

Here is something little.

Up it comes.

10

Oh, my. Oh, my.

It is big, big, big.

I can go up.

See me go up.

Up, up, up and away.

12

Look here, look here.

I see a house.

It is a big, big house.

I want to go in.

In I go.

Jump, jump, jump.

It is big in here.

It is big for little me.

15

Here is something.

It is not big.

It is little and red.

16

Look, look.

It can work.

It can make something.

Come to me.

Come to me.

I want you.

Come to my house.

Away we go.

Oh, look here.

Here is something for Mother.

Something for my mother.

And here is something.

We can play it.

We can make it play.

It is fun to play.

Come, come.

Come to my house.

Come to my mother.

Here we go.

Away, away, away.

Oh, my.

Here comes something.

Something big.

Where can I go?

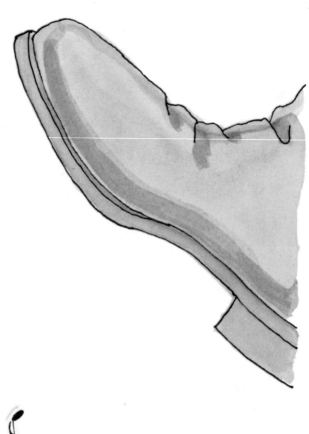

Help, help.

Here I go.

Run, run, run.

And here I go.

Down, down, down.

Mother, Mother.

Here I come.

Help me. Help me.

We can work.

We can make it come down.

Here, Mother.

Here is something for you.

Margaret Hillert, author of several books in the MCP Beginning-To-Read Series, is a writer, poet, and teacher.

The Magic Beans

Delightful illustrations accompany this favorite tale of Jack and the Beanstalk which is told in 44 preprimer words.

Word List

7	oh		in		to
	look	**10**	and		jump
	here		see	**15**	for
	is		up	**16**	not
	something		it	**17**	work
	funny		comes		make
	one	**11**	my	**18**	you
	red		big		we
	blue	**12**	I	**19**	mother
	yellow		can	**20**	play
8	little		me		fun
	two		away	**23**	where
	three	**13**	a	**24**	help
9	go		house		run
	down	**14**	want		